NEGATIVE VOL.1

CHODI.DHAMAR RAJ
SANTOSH

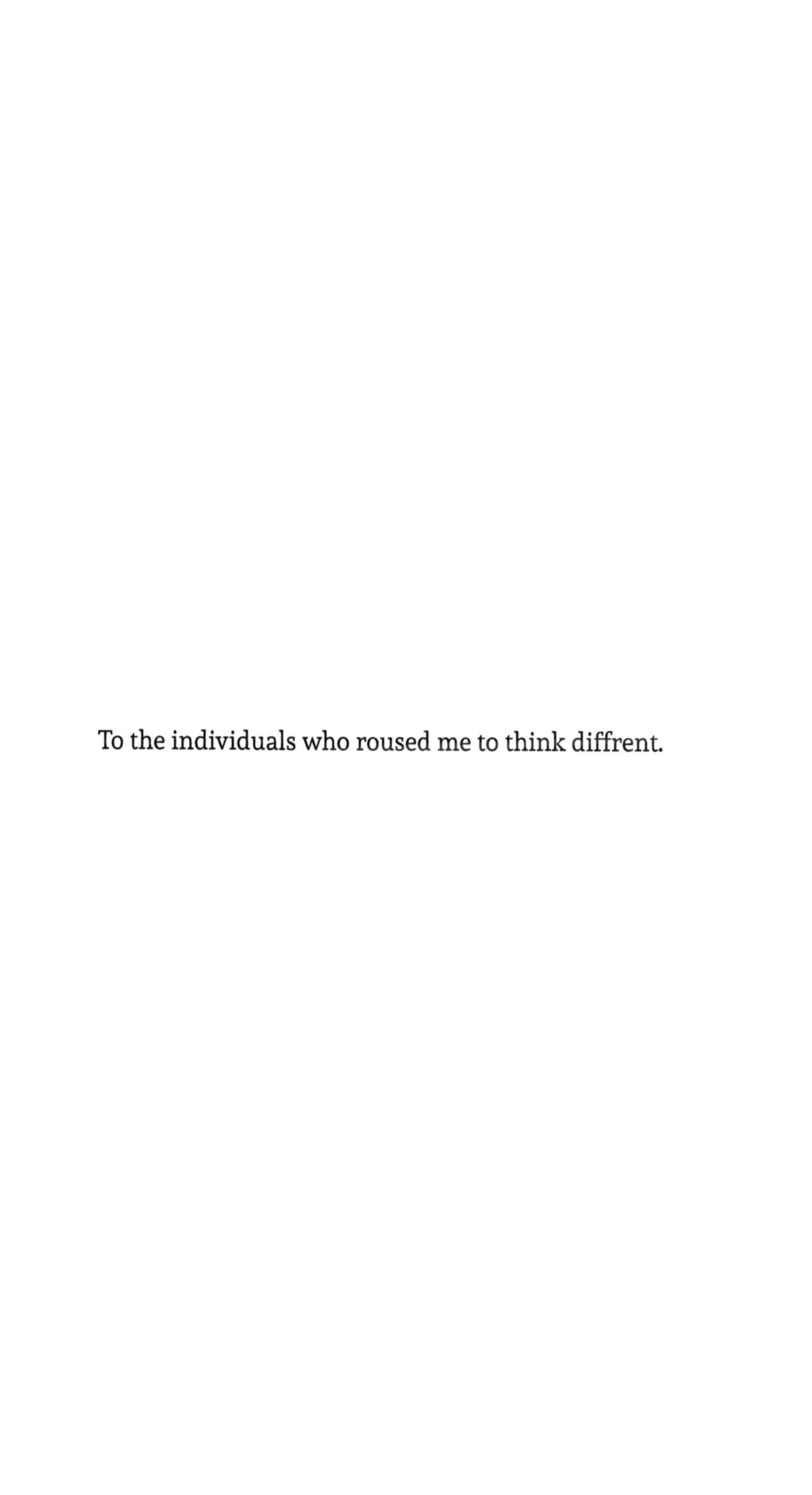

To the individuals who roused me to think diffrent.

Contents

FOREWORD

This book is absolutely fictitious .

This book isn't connected with any religion , local area ,or any individual

PREFACE

Breakups are the most terrible phases of our life, but when you study children, they too have feelings,they too get hurt, but they move on so quickly that they forget, they forgive, and they have a question for everything, regardless of what we say.

They think in numerous ways, and interacting with them helped me get over my post-breakup sorrow.

They also inspired me to examine everything and think about things in new ways, which motivated me to write this book.

Acknowledgements

I might want to pass my unique thanks on to my friend Teja and my cousin Jaya for empowering me to distribute my considerations.

Secondly, I might likewise want to thank my parents and my sister for being strong to me constantly.

Prologue

As I previously stated, the inspiration for this book came to me when I began spending time with children. I began addressing everything and imagining what might have occurred if things had gone differently And I picked the word Negative as title of the book since it would be about thinking in reverse, about several things. .And the excursion into composing this book was so fun and simple as it was generally fictitious. And the journey of the book started because once one child ask for me to tell him a tale, and I began narrating him old stories that I had read or listened then he got bored and that made me to envision this story and that considerations drove me to make the characters of Alex, Asard, Remiras thus on....

I

THE BEGINNING

It was 12 at night the streets were unoccupied ,only thing i can hear is that

the street dogs barking sound, i was in a bit hurry , by tomorrow morning i must attend an interview i was unable to find a cab near me i was walking in a hurry to reach the train station. The streets were fully covered with fog i went on walking and reached the train station the train had already arrived on to the platform , i boarded the train in a hurry , the train started moving there is no one in the train. I felt tired after a long walk to the station , I decided to have a small nap and I slowly had a snoring tight sleep sometime later it seemed like something knocked me so hard, I am too drowsy I opened my eyes , can't see anything. it was all dark i tried to to move but my hands were tied . and my eyes were blind folded

i can sense someone around me ,

someone unfolded my eyes he is tall with broad shoulders looked like a wrestler , and my bag with the documents was in his hands, I screamed for help, but there is no one in the compartment except me and him , he punched me in the face i was bleeding i controlled my anger with no other option . I thought he was doing this for the money so I offered money to him, he stood silent I offered again but he didn't responded.

After a few minutes with a loud voice he said his name was the victor. I asked him why he is doing this he kicked on my belly and said that he should only ask the questions and I must answer them .

"I know you must attend an interview by the morning the train will reach your destination within 6 hours" victor said .

"how did you know that ? why are you doing this" i questioned him

he kicked me again and said that he should only question.

i requested him to set me free, victor said that he would definatly set me free if i could impress him.

what? i questioned .

"did you ever heard off vikram betal stories iam gonna tell you some stories and at the end of each one i will ask you a question if you could impress me with your answer i am going to set you free" victor replaid.

" Are you screwing with me? what if i say im not intrested in playing games with you " i yelled.

" it is as simple as iam going to shoot you in the head and find some other to play " Victor murmured to my ear.

" you are a psychopath " i told him

victor beat me to the pulp , he dragged me on to the floor ,my shirt was torn a part without further choice i said yes to play with him.

my locket went out hanging around my neck.

"Oh an image of the gods in your locket, you look devout. ok we go easy weezy i will narrate you a story about god

"Victor said with a terrible laughter.

victor's narration

year 5050

300 years ahead from here. this was a story about a man named Alex. he is working as a soldier in earth protection force till year 5050 earth is having only 3 nations greed had destroyed the mother nature and earth had lost its beauty , later the remaining 3 nations collectively formed earth protection force and from past few days earth had been continuously attacked by unknown creatures coming out from nowhere killing people and destroying cities.

"Like everything you do now" i interrupted him.

i thought he would beat me again but he smiled and continued nerating

time midnight 2:45 AM temprature was stone cold with dim fog all around, Alex and his team were on duty Alex was playing with mascot his trained dog, his squad were having coffee to battle cold Alex and mascot went few steps away from the camp

for urination Alex unzipped his phant and started taking a leak all of a sudden mascot began to bark and went running back to camp Alex cleared his bladder and walked back to the camp.

As Alex approached, he was shocked that his team was lying breathless and bleeding to death,

Alex looked all around, he tried to contact for backup, but the radio was dead

mascot started barking again,he came out of the tent, then he realized that he was surrounded by those mysterious creatures from all sides

Alex's adrenaline was rushing he loaded his riffle and started shooting them hours passed, they kept on coming Alex continued shooting at them, but they were still coming out of nowhere, Alex was out of ammo at last he unpinned the grenade he tossed it on to those creatures tragically mascot went hunting those creatures and died because of the grenade explosion.

Alex's heart was weighing more than any measure with grief for losing his squad and mascot. He continued hand-to-hand fighting for hours and collapsed in the middle of the fight. Seven hours later he opened his eyes and had no idea where he was. It was all white around him and there appeared an angel in white dress before him.

"Why aren't women on earth as beautiful as angels in the sky," Alex asked.

"You are not dead, it is not paradise I am a nurse you are at the hospital" the lady replied.

"Oh no alive again, " said Alex with frustration.

"What does that mean, aren't you happy that you survived," the nurse asked.

"Not so much" Alex replays disappointingly.

The nurse felt so different about Alex's behavior, she thought he was out of his mind. She asked him why? He is not happy and surprised to be alive.

"not much surprised it happens every time, " Alex replied

"what happens?" nurse questioned .

"I encountered death many times before no matter what happens I survive. When I was 8 years old I was kidnapped and they forcibly made me and other children to work in a chemical factory.

One day the leakage in the pipes caused the fire in the plant all the children died except one. Later I was taken to the orphanage and I studied well, I joined police forces when I was 21.

One night, some hooligans broke into my house, they started firing me, I survived, and my girlfriend died.And later I was promoted to the Earth Protection Force and deployed to the Mariana Trench. The opposite forces gave us an ambush.

I took a bullet in my head and I survived after a surgery "Alex explained

"You are lucky" the nurse said

"do you really think it's lucky to lose loved ones and live again and again?" Alex asked disppointedly

Nurse advised Alex to stop thinking as he needed rest she gave him an injection and he again went back to sleep.

Alex got discharged from hospital with a breathing body and baggage of depression.

Having returned back to his house, he rearranged things. He missed his team so much he loved his mascot. He trained him he fed him and he lost him to forget all this. Alex tried to watch television but he got bored very soon. He also played video games but they too couldn't make him ignore the pain. He tried all other ways to forget but they didn't work this time. Later the next day Alex had some alcohol to get out of the grief

"tring tring" door bell rang

Alex opened the door and it was the nurse. He welcomed her in, he offered her a coffee. When Alex walked into the kitchen, the nurse noticed a vodka glass on the table. And got mad

"we are trying to help you recover and you are having alcohol" the nurse yelled

"Sorry, I am unable to get out of mental pain.I tried everything and at last. i tried alcohol " explained Alex.

"if you really want to get out of the depression stop having it and read a worthwhile book" Advised the nurse.

Later, she gave him an injection and she left Alex felt so dizzy after having it that he slept till the evening. When he woke up he thought about buying a book. However, he decided to buy a printed book. In the year 5050, it is so expensive and challenging to get a printed hard copy book. Alex had a shower and wiped dust off his air bike. He started the engine and drove to the book market. He asked the salesman to show some best fiction books. He showed him a lot of books but nothing attracted Alex. After searching a lot of books for an hour at last Alex found a very old book with the title "something you need to know" he got a strange feeling by seeing it.Alex asked the salesman to pack that book he purchased it he paid for it and received an electronic bill. He returned home with the book he placed it on the table had dinner and slept for that night. Later the next morning he opened the book. There was nothing written on the first page, no author's name, no page numbers. He turned over the page and on the second page it was written that

"a message to Alex"

Alex felt a bit strange he thought that the name would be a coincidence.He turned over the page and started reading

II

THE DAIRY OF THE DEVIL

The book says

"long long ago so long ago before the beginning of the beginning, there was nothing except a couple namely Frey and Bragie. They both were together for billions of billion years there was nothing no planets, no stars,no galaxies, no universes, except Frey and Bragie the space was empty it was darkness all around Bragie started feeling bored after all these years nothing around except darkness. Frey noticed Bragie getting bored and when she was in sleep he created planets, stars, moons, galaxies and universes. So on.. and made space as a beautiful place to surprise Bragie. Bragie was full of joy. She kept on watching those beautiful shapes and lights of planets, satellites and stars and she started to roam all around the space with joy and happiness. She always used to re-arrange planets, stars and moons in a beautiful manner. She did it for trillions of years

At one point Frey and Bragie were spending some quality time together.

They were talking and in the middle of the talk Bragie thanked Frey for making her happy by making space a more attractive place. Her response was that she liked those planets, stars, etc. Very much and she had the impression that there was still something missing in the work. She mentioned that she wished to bring life into the cosmos. Frey was astonished after hearing that, and with a blended feeling of dread and outrage he escaped the bed and he got out of the bed. Bragie asked frey that why did he dismissed the idea of makinglife

"My love, you know, we creators can easily construct any shape and size, but in order to generate life, we must first create gods, and they alone have the capacity to create life" Frey answered.

"Why don't we produce them?" Bragie inquired.

"In order to produce them, we must transmit our own life and force, which means we will perish."

Frey replied with outrage.By stating this, Frey requested the Bragie to forget about the concept of developing life. Bragie afterwards took on rounds to monitor all the universes, as she did every now and again, but her yearning to produce life had grown like a tumour. a ton of tim

This time, Bragie did not return home; instead, she chose to create life by handing on the power of her soul to create gods. Frey began his hunt throughout all worlds in search of Bragie.

Knock knock someone knocked on the door,

it was the medical attendant again, When Alex approached the door, it was unlocked when his retina was scanned.He invited her in,he offer her espresso and he made espresso for them

"I'm sorry till now I didnt even asked your name " said Alex "gracious its is Diana " the attendant replayed

she inspected Alex recuperation and she gave him the infusion once more After the injection, Alex felt a little woozy.

"better than anyone might have expected I attempted your instruct regarding getting a decent book, I brought a fascinating book i hooked me for hours and im still reading" " Alex commented.

Alex gave the book to Diana she kept it a side and continued to converse with alex because of the infusion alex was feeling excessively drowsy and he dozed off in the middle of conversation.

"how do you feel now?" Diana asked

He woke up after 30 minutes

"I'm sorry I made you stand by I got into rest unwittingly " Alex apolozised

"It's alright I don't psyche " Diana replaid.

Alex apologized to her and inquired if she had read the book or not.

Diana stated, "It was a very entertaining novel with a lot of humour."

"what? that isnt a humor book it is a made up spine chiller" Alex asked shockingly.

He opened the book and attempted to demonstrate it to Diana, and it was all different, there is a humor in it was not the story that he read earlier .He got frantic in the wake of watching a whole diffrent story in the book; even the title of the book got changed.

"are you all right"asked Diana

He required a couple of moments to escape the shock.

"indeed I'm fine" Alex replaid.

"ineed to go now alex" Diana said

"how did you came here?" Alex enquired

" I took an air taxi to reach here" she replaid

"you got late only because of me if you don't mind I will drop you at the emergency clinic on my air bike please don't say no" Alex made a request.

He took her on his air motorbike by while they were on their way. Alex's cerebrum was hustling with considerations; such countless inquiries had arisen in his mind.

In the wake of dropping her without saying bye he surged back to his home he opened the book it was not the same old narrative, he shut it again opened it again and he did this for many times, he is god frantic the throwed every one of the items near him because of his indignation.

He re-started his bike and sped to the book market, he proceeded to the same shop where he bought the book, and he called the salesperson in a hurry.

"Sir, how may I assist you?" The salesperson inquired.

"Could you please get a copy of book the "SOMETHING YOU NEED TO KNOW" for me?" Alex inquired.

The salesperson apologised, "sorry sir, we don't have that book here."

Alex said, "Are they out of stock?"

"No sir, we don't sell any book with that name here," the

salesperson explained.

by paying attention to him alex out seethed and said that he carried a book with that name from here, and alex pulled up his mobile and showed the bill for that book to the salesman.

The salesperson examined the bill.

"Sorry sir, but you requested for another book; the book in this bill is accessible here,

but you stated another name; you may be wrong; I'll get the book in this bill right now," the salesman said.

The salesperson took out a funny book and placed it in front of Alex, who screamed angrily at him.

""What are you messing around" Alex shouted.

"Sir, I brought the exact book that was on the bill," stated the salesperson.

Alex viewed the bill and, surprisingly, the bill got transformed; it was not a similar name in the bill.

He admonished the salesperson, apologized profusely, and exited the store

Alex returned back home loaded with disarray, he is having a serious cerebral pain, he attempted to recall everything from beginning, and at a point he recalled the page number 2 in the book, it was composed that "a message to Alex" then, at that point, he understood that this book Is intended to peruse simply by Alex he went close to the book one final time and gradually opened page number 2 the words reworked as "this message is just for you ALex" he can't really accept that what he is seeing everything felt like a fantasy to him however later he came to his sense and felt glad for the story re showed up.

Alex began reading the book right away.

THE BOOK

Bragie changed the energy of her spirit into life-making gods. And set certain conditions for them. She started delivering them by transferring her spirit energy. The divine beings were being created and her spirit is getting frail, as she is gradually evaporating.

The circumstances were

* All divine beings earlier obligation is to make life, and keep up with life.

*Despite the fact that they were prevalent creatures, they won't be the

immortals,but they can be everlastingly with an opportunity ,by their

eternality would be interlinked with their purpose. Divine beings won't

have demise until they preserve the last life of any

planet,star,moon,etc.. be that as it may, once assuming, no life exists there

will be no divine beings. Also, the powers and strength of divine beings would

additionally, be straightforwardly relative to the number of inhabitants in life.if life expands, divine beings would develop more strength and power if the life

starts to diminish, they will gradually begin losing their

strength and powers.

* divine beings should deal with their militaries and satisfy their

needs to keep them faithful

Bragie created 60 distinct divine beings with various obligations and their 60 million militaries of evech she said every one of the principles and conditions to divine beings, and she is disappearing into air gradually.

A few significant gods

REIMRAS is the oldest of divine beings and savvies and incomparable head of gods. His obligation is to lead divine beings in making life and keeping up with life.

TYRONK is the lord of strength, the fiercest of all gods, although he is arrogant and overconfident.

IIGOF is the goddess assigned to keep a track on developments of the universes and to orchestrate the objects of universe as per the circumstances.

GERSELLA the goddess of affection and harmony

HERTHAGA the goddess of time.

HEIOSTA the goddess of death.

JIANEIR the lord of wizardry

also other excess different divine beings were made

While Bragie was slowly evaporating, Frey searched the worlds for her, and when he found her, she had vanished into thin air. Frey rushed towards her, attempting to catch her, but she vanished straight in front of his eyes, leaving him helpless. Distressed by the unbearable agony, he screamed.

Hardly any developments passed, as divine beings went close to Frey, and they informed that they were leaving divine beings turned around to leave.

"Wait," Frey replied, his voice strained.

Divine beings halted.

"You were formed by Bragie surrendering her soul to fulfil her passion to create life,and you divine beings should do that"

Frey said.

" you dont need to recollect us our obligation we know what to do"

Trylonk replaid with self-importance.

Frey said that they should make life within 10 billion

years else all divine beings would be turned to dust .Frey had set an

a certain time restriction for their obligation.

Later, divine beings moved away. Frey stayed there and continued to cry.

The divine beings began to scan a spot for themselves as well as their militaries to remain.

Furthermore, they chose a spot they had built a wonderful luxuriant paradise for themselves as well as their militaries. They had spent 5 billion years fulfilling their requirements and building paradise.

Also, Reimras recalled the state of frey to make life inside in 5 billion years, as he coordinated an opening ceremony at the regal corridor of the paradise. All divine beings attended the gathering.

"dear individuals from the paradise we had developed a lovely spot for ourselves and presently we need to make life for our sustainabilty as all of you know our lifes are interlinked with our obligation and we as a whole should celebrate for building this excellent paradise" said Reimras.

The gods rejoiced, they opened the wine casks and began the ceremony.

All divine beings cheered with satisfaction. They opened the wine barrels and began the ceremony.

Then, at that point, a tremendous lightning out of nowhere arrived at paradise. All divine beings vision got obscured. They had cleared their eyes, and afterward there seemed a gigantic character with a brown complexion, as like a foreboding shadow, his eyes were all red like a consuming star tone. He seemed quite frightening.

He approached near Reimras's throne and he introduced himself as Asard and said that his work was to help divine beings in making life. And enquired the divine beings how far they had accomplished the work of making life.

"we are going to begin"said Reimras

"what you haven't start the work yet and every one of you are hosting a party how reckless you are Frey and Bragie Frey and Bragie gave life and immortality to us, and you had forgotten your obligations and were enjoying,"said Asard with a disturbing tone

With in a squint of time, Reimras entered his super vision and he saw. Frey continued to cry for 5 billion years sitting at a similar place where Bragie disappeared he continued to cry and cry however his pity and agony of losing Bragie never left him and 2 years back frey concluded that he doesn't need his existence without Bragie he imagined that assuming if he can make 60 additional divine beings by forfeiting his spirit the bragie's desire can be satisfied a whole lot earlier so he began the most common way of making divine beings he initially remembered to make 60 divine beings yet he was in brimming with sorrow his feelings were out of control, he let completely go over his brain and he accidentally made one god (Asard) with the combined strength of all 60 gods to be created and he inferred just a single obligation on Asard that to help god's in making life and no more obligations , Asard was straightforwardly immortal. By observing this, Reimras got shocked .and just the beneficial thing he saw was that Asard was unaware of the mystery of god's immortality and its connection to life..

Reimras awoke from his super vision. Furthermore With the shock, he stood up, Asard continued to question the divine beings regarding how they would make life, and where might they initially present the life, and what plans they were had for it. While keeping the discussion going, Remimras continued to respond to Asard .He was as yet in shock while keeping the discussion going as Asard took his seat on the ultimate throne. This enraged Reimras to the point of wrath, but knowing Asard's might, he kept his cool, and didn't display his rage.

While the two of them were conversing, Tyronk interjected and ordered Asard to get from the throne.

"it was uniquely for the head of divine beings you cant sit there"Tyronk said with disdain.

" alright why not"Asard replayed nonchalantly

Furthermore, he got out of the throne.

"Alright presently show a spot in paradise for myself as well as my fellows to stay"asked Asard.

"How could you expect that?" Tyronk said, disgusted.

"what's wrong did i asked"Asard questioned

Jianeir, Lord of Wizardry, fashioned a mirror copy of Asard and his companions and presented it to him.

"what does it mean"Asard confusingly inquired

"Your appearance, as well as that of your compatriots, is horribly unattractive. Heaven is a lovely place, and we, the gods created by Bragie, were a mirror of her beauty. and you and your comrades were a mirror of Frey's misery, and how can we let such ugliness into this lovely heaven? "Tyronk repeated it in a cringe-worthy tone.

All gods started laughing at Asard.

Asard snatched Jianeir's neck, and slung him away. Jianeir flying right towards the Reimras, crashed the throne.Tyronk punched the Asard in his face asard didn't move. He stood like a statue Tyronk kept on punching just then. Asard catches the hand of Tyronk he gave a blow on to the chest of Tyronk then Tyronk went on bouncing, crashing the pillars of the royal hall just within a few seconds, most of the royal hall collapses . Tyronk hauled his weapon out of his holster Asard grinned both went running towards each watching this each god encountered the dread for the first time the two of them were coming close and the Reimras entered the center of the battle he apologized Asard in the interest of Tyronk's conduct, and ordered Tyronk to venture back

Both quieted down .

Reimras summoned his staff and ordered them to show Asard and his companions lodgings.

" no thanks I will discover some other spot we would rather not be here in a spot like trash "said Asard

He and his army marched away, threatening the gods to commence the process of creating life in only one day.

"Ultimate leader, why did you stop me, I would have served him a lesson," Tyronk exclaimed angrily after Asard had left.

"great joke yet I am not in a temperament to giggle presently do you think I am out of psyche to leave somebody who sat on my throne before me " said Reimras, blasting out his resentment.

"My lord, he insulted us; we must seek our revenge on evil," Jainieir continued, "and you are still mute; what is the matter?"

Reimras strolled upto his throne and he sat back on it.

He revealed to the gods what he had seen with his super vision concerning Asard.

by realizing that Asard was straightforwardly unfading and his power divine beings astounded

"no divine beings should provoke him everyone should maintain peace with Asard" commanded Remiras.

And that was the end of the ceremony.

Later, Remiras ordered the gods to begin the task of making life.

"this is offending we are the incomparable and you,our pioneer got scared to that

vile creature and following his order"Tyronk said with bothering

"Mind your words, Tyronk," the Reimras warned.

"I'm sorry my master however this is annoying " Tyronk said.

"I know , I'm not doing this since that he cautioned us to start.you know as life builds our powers also expands Asard might be stronger than us for the time being nevertheless we increment our capacity to any degree by expanding the life in the universes " Remiras said astutely .

Goddess Iigof went to look for an appropriate planet for introducing life. In thc meantime Asard was on his way, searching for a spot to remain. Both encountered a planet with special component water framed of Frey's tears: when frey sobbed for a very long time, his tears went streaming to certain planets, and one of it was planet varth and Asard chose to remain on varth he began developing his fortress on planet earth without realizing this Iigof analyzed the planet varth and she returned to heaven and informed divine beings that she encountered a planet that is effectively reasonable for living. Divine beings began the most common way of making living creatures.

initially divine beings acquainted unicellular organisms on with the planet varth followed by little measured creatures and greater creatures. The organisms reproduced their children on Varth, and the planet grew increasingly beautiful day by day. Gods noticed that as life increased, so did their powers, so they continued to produce life. Later, they noticed that the more advanced forms of life they introduced, the more power they gained. and they began working on a more complex version of life (the humans)

Divine beings began to make people they had wrapped up making the main couple in particular Lucy and Goden divine beings fitted the high level minds into the collection of them and they were prepared to send off on to varth before sending them on to varth divine beings gave some guidelines to them.

The guidlines

*their minds would be shut down during the excursion from heaven to varth and their cerebrums would get activated once they arrived at the varth, the two of them would be arrived on different place from another and they should look for one another and they should get hitched and the second couple would be shipped off to varth following seven days from that point. Later the two couples should get their youngsters married to increment the human populace

Both Lucy and Goden arrived on to varth their brains got activated after some time of reaching varth then they remembered the instructions to them they searched for one another and later a week they met each other they got married. Gods watched this from a higher place and they affirmed that the experiment worked they sent off the second couple immediately to be specific Icy and Tom these two were likewise given the equivalent guidelines both of their minds were shut down and they were shipped off to varth and presently happened the greatest turn in the story Icy was launched where Asard was relaxing, the two of them looked each other Icy was pretty much as wonderful as the bright moonlight Asard was staggered taking a gander at her excellence he stood like a sculpture watching at her Icy was additionally gazing directly at Asard the two of them experienced passionate feelings for one another Asard took her with him and acquainted her as his sovereign with his devotees then her cerebrum got actuated she recollected her guidelines yet she overlooked them as she was enamored with Asard now.

Without realising it, Tom went on a quest for Icy around the Varth, but he couldn't locate her anywhere. At one point he was out of energy, and afterward he saw a jackass and he requested that it help him .The jackass consented to help Tom yet with a condition that Tom should wed the jackass too.....and the Tom agreed...so they married, and the donkey let Tom ride on its back while they looked for Icy.

Icy and Asard went to the ocean side for a walk Asard went into the sea keeping in touch with his maker's tears as they make him more reinforce Icy was looking out for the banks of the sea, then, at that point, showed up Tom riding the jackass .Tom Tom forced Icy to come along with him and marry him, but she refused.However, Icy denied it and clarified all that happened. Tom then forcibly tried to take Icy away she opposed yet Tom lifted her and put her on his jackass then, at that point, Arrived asard from the sea and watching Tom constraining Icy he cut off his hand and Tom fled screamingly with torment.

Then Icy informed Asard of all that had happened, and she was terrified.

"dont stress now you are mine I will chat with divine beings

In the event that they come for you, I won't let you go, my

affection " gaureented Asard.

Shouting with the torment of losing his hand, Tom went to meet Godan. He asked the Godan to assist him with battling the Asard.Both Godan and Tom went walking towards the Asards stronghold. Yet when they arrived there after seeing Asard, they shuddered with dread and returned without articulating a word. Then following not many days, Iigof came for rounds and sensed something was wrong, so then she attempted to find all the people with her super sense. she found 3 of them and she couldn't find Icy then she showed up before

The remaining humans, then they disclosed everything that had happened to them. She took the three of them alongside her by imagining that there might be a danger to them from Asard.

By seeing people with Iigof in paradise, Reimras got baffled, and he asked Iigof for what valid reason she carried them to heaven. And she disclosed everything that happened to them in the wake of paying attention to her. Remiras said that he would take care of the circumstances, and asked people to leave. But Tom denied as he got terrified by Asard, he asked to safeguard him until the circumstances quiets down. Reimras acknowledged his solicitation and asked to remain at the paradise guests room and cautioned him to stay out of any other rooms. Godan and Lucy were sent back to varth. Godan was taken to the guests lobby later at Royal Hall. Divine beings were having a discussion.

"Iigof what have you done ! without disscussing anything with us how is it that you could straightforwardly carried somebody to paradise" Reimras cautioned.

" I am sorry my master I committed an error in a rush I thought there would a danger to them"Iigof said.

"Jianeir I request you to fabricate tremendous magic gates

for paradise

that nobody could enter it without our approval." said

Reimras.

"indeed my chief said" Jianeir

"What about Asard and Icy, my lord? If he had a child with Icy, the child would be eternal, just like Asard.and their youngsters and their kids so on will be the immortals. And if humans become immortal as well,, we will lose our dominance.

ahh.. My head is impacting.you shouldn't have called a halt to the battle that day."Tryronk opined.

"we might be powerful than before yet at the same time we must be carefull

until we foster more strength and power, we need to bargain.

this circumstance in a strategic manner." said Reimras.

"how" asked confounded Tyronk

"getting ill will with Asard isn't so fine better we welcome him and Icy to remain with us in paradise so the human folk won't be immortals" said Reimras.

Tyronk stormed out of the room, enraged, after hearing this.

Goddess Herthaga sitting at a corner grinned, observing this.

The following morning all divine beings with the exception of Tyronk went down to varth. Also they met Asard. also they congratulated on his marriage to Icy.

"I was worried that gods would be furious because I disobeyed your commands, but I am so delighted you forgave me and came down to meet me, my lord,"Icy communicated her joy.

Asard organized celebrate with the divine beings, and keeping in mind that having their lunch, Reimras requested that Asard and Icy return to paradise and remain with them.

"Much obliged for welcoming me sibling but with darkness, me and my comrades will grow stronger. Heaven is a place of brightness.It will be more brilliant 100% of the time there, however here varth is having constantly during night it was generally dim and we need that," denyingly said Asard "we can make paradise excessively hazier during nights"Reimras offered

"why such a difficult situation to you I'm fine here and I had appended a passionate holding with this spot." Asard said again denyingly

"consider it again my sibling since we are building doors to paradise once in the event that they complete development nobody can enter paradise with the exception of the individuals from paradise come and go along with us before it"said Jaineir.

Even still, Asard declined their invitation.

divine beings began their excursion back to paradise.

soon thereafter divine beings were having a beverage at paradise's bar

"I realize he would dismiss your proposition now the people will likewise be equivalents to all of us .happenned beacause of that Frey he made that awful animal Asard and Asard is making problems"said Tyronk.

"quit agonizing and thoroughly consider what to do know"Reimras said

"Nothing in our hands anymore, it's all done," Jariner expressed his dissatisfaction.

they continued to have one more galss of wine over and over parcel of time elapsed they disscussed everything occurred .

kr... Kr.... the bar door slowly opened, making a tiny noise.

Jaineir yelled, "Who is that?"

Then Tom arrived, slowly saying "it's me my lord"

"How dare you enter here, who let you in?" Tyronk snarled.

"How dare you enter here, who let you in?" Tyronk raged. "Did you hear anything?" Reimras inquired. "Nothing, my lord, save the secret regarding gods' immortality," Tom said deftly.

"What????" said the Reimras

"My lord, I am a loyal human for you, and I will not tell anybody about it. I was passing by the bar when I heard your conversations, and if I wanted to betray you, I could have gone back to the guests room after hearing all of this, but I am here to demonstrate my loyalty to you.I'm here to introduce you a prompt my divine beings" Tom said.

"Why should we listen to an inferior like you?" Tyronk said.

"let him speak" Reimras said.

"my rulers Asard isn't just an issue for you he additionally embarrassed me as well and I'm having an arrangement

to obliterate him.
Dear masters he wedded Icy and you atteneded their gathering as well" Tom said.

"Then what should we do?""Wait for them to have babies and babysit them?" Tyronk grumbled.

"no my ruler you as of now discusssed some time back that frey made Asard when frey was in tragic mental state then we can win Asard with sadness"Tom replayed

"how? " addressed Jaineir

"Asard is everlasting and he cannot be killed by any others .yet Icy was not an immortal and you made her. let Asard connect his psychological holding with Icy for certain days and kill her before she concieve her child then Asard comes hurrying to divine beings he initially undermine's you to resurrect her later he even begs you, and then gods must still say there is no way to bring a dead soul back to life. he will turn out to be intellectually weak then remind him that creatures on varth were made with a particular life expectancy and they will definatly bite the dust after their time is finished. What's more presently let him know little lie there would be only a solitary technique for bringing a dead human is that any god should relinquish their time everlasting and their heart ought to be squashed close by the soul material of the dead human and with that structure they can again make a comparable human .by waiting patiently, standing by listening to this Asard will take out his jewel heart out and hands over it to divine creatures then you know what to do "savvy Tom explained.

"Why would Asard do that just for a woman?" asked Heiosta.

"Assuming her beauty can make a man wed a donkey," Then it can make Asard give up his gem heart, "said Tom with a finesse grin.

The gods were enthralled by the concept.

Both Icy and Asard had spent a lot of time together and one day Icy got pregnant . Both of them were lying in bed. They talked for quite a long time and dozed off that night. The following morning the sun was up, yet Icy was resting Asard went out without disturbing her. He returned after a while, yet Icy was dozing. It was again half light, but still, she wouldn't awaken Asard attempted to wake her. However she wasn't moving. Asard was confounded, then he heard a murmuring sound. He turned around, and it was the Heiosta.

"how hard you might attempt she wont be awaken" said Heiosta.

"why?" asked Asard.

"On Varth, life forms were made with a particular future in , and they will surely kick the bucket when their time is up.Heiosta "would you be able to bring her back"Asard inquired.

"I'm goddess of death I cannot assist you with better ask

Remiras, he may help you, "said Heiosta.

Heiosta clarified the significance of death to Asard, and she vanished.

Asard picked Icy's body in his arms and he began his excursion to paradise with a lightning speed Asard was feeling his psychological aggravation he is getting more fragile he arrived at the doors of paradise he attempted to enter however the can't overcome them as the mysterious entryways doesn't permitted him, he coercively attempted to enter yet each time he enters the entryways landed him into a different place each time he was landed into a different area he flied back to the doors over and over he attempted to enter yet no use atlast Asard was finished with it and he plunked down in front of the entryways and yelled for Remiras finally the doors opened and Remiras came out .When Asard saw him, he went running toward him and asked him for help.

"that cant be done it was inconceivable" said Remiras.

"however, Heiosta said you could help me . please" asked Asard.

"indeed yet I dont want this to be finished by that way "said Remiras "what was that way kindly clarify" Asard enquired

"Icy's soul has been already destroyed but we still have her soul material there would be only a solitary technique for bringing a dead human is that any god would give up their eternal time and their heart to be squashed close by the soul material of the dead human. And with that structure they can again make a comparable human.." said Remiras.

After paying attention to Remiras immediately, Asard shut his eyes and raised all his unfading enhancer to his heart. His chest started to sparkle that resembled a consuming star, and he culled his precious stone heart out of his body, and he gave it to Reimras. And he returned..

Thump somebody thumped the door Alex was perusing interestingly with a disturbing face he shut the book and he went close to the entryway it checked his retina and opened the door and afterward he saw those animals that assaulted him at the camp he immediately shut the entryway and brought his riffle out and he opened entryway again yet there is presently outside.

again, Alex continued reading, but what Alex doesn't know is that those creatures entered the house and were behind him while he was reading..

THE BOOK SAYS

Asard returned to varth in the wake of giving over his gem heart.

"What an idiot, let's murder that filthy beast right now," Tyronk said.

"why so speedy" said Reimras

They all went in side the paradise and Reimras put Asard's heart in the focal storage of the paradise Tyronk assaigned 30,000 soldiers to guard the storage and Jainer made an enchanted insurance to their storage and later they went into the paradise's lab and the workers brought the confined soul of Icy and they re introduced her spirit into her body but they had cleared all her memories.

She was a completely different person now.

Reimras asked the workers to call Tom when Tom arrived there Reimras ordered Tom to leave back to varth, and to wait at the tallest peak of the varth. Tom followed the instructions and he did the same. And gods gave same old instructions to Icy and they shut her brain and this time they dropped her on the the tallest peak of varth where Tom was waiting Icy landed on to varth and she found Tom there and as per instruction when Tom asked her hand, she gave it to him immediately, Tom arranged their wedding, meanwhile, Tyronk reached earth and visited Asard.

"I thought you loved her so much " said Tyronk.

Asard said "yes" with a deep sarrow

"then what are you still doing here we gods gave her re birth

After a lot of effort we have already dropped her on the

tallest peak of varth go and find her" said Tyronk.

"thank you very my and i appolozise you for the fight" said Asard

Asard's happiness flooded, he thanked Tyronk, and immediately he alone ran towards the tallest peak on varth leaving all his army behind. But when he reached there he saw the heart-burning scene Icy, being close to Tom Asard, shouted with all his pain and feelings by listening to it Icy went hiding behind the shoulders of Tom. She remembers nothing, he drove his weapon towards Tom, and bang, something blocked him. Asard was surprised to see Remiras blocking him. Tyronk attacked from behind

"We gods wont let you kill our creation" said Remiras.

"but" said Asard

And Jaineir tied Asard with his magic ropes.

Asard looked straight into the eyes of Icy. She moved her sight away, and the outraged Asard Asard turned into a huge dark scary form and broke the ropes. He knocked Tyronk on to his knees and slashed his head. but again, Tyronk's head regenerated, "we are immortals you insect do you think you can finish me off" said Tyronk.

"if in that case all of you would be fighting me and keep getting hurt forever"said Asard

mean while Asard's fellows reached there, Asard and his armies made gods feel the pain and taught them to scream with pain. Asard kept on killing, but they came back again and again

"he is just a mortal but yet we cant reach our swords to his throat we must finish him of before its dark "said Remiras.

Jaineir created illusions of Icy and shifted the Asards concentration from the battlefield, and then from back Tyronk slashed the Asard's head.

When the strong Asard finally fell, his breath came to an end. Later, the Asards' general Fresaiz led the fight, and they fought for vengeance. The sky turned dark. They took advantage of this, and they got stronger with darkness to deal with them. Iigof arranged for the moon to provide light to planet Varth at night, and the Asard's army began to lose ground, fleeing and hiding in dark areas. The gods returned to heaven, glad of their triumph over Asard.

The gods celebrated their victory over Asard, and it was all calmed down, the gods were peaceful, and then one day the Icy stomach started to get bigger and with tension she went in hurry to Tom and she informed him and he too can't figure out why it was getting bigger and then they went to Lucy for help and then Lucy confirmed that Icy was carrying her baby Icy went soo happy after listening to this but Godan was out of his mind because it just passed 2 months hardly after their marriage and how can she carry a baby so quick. Then he left Icy alone, and he left,

And after a month Iigof came on rounds to planet varth then she found Icy crying Iigof stopped for a while and enquired Icy the reason for why she is crying Icy explained it to Iigof, and after listening to it she went back to heaven and informed gods about the issue, The gods then researched the matter and discovered that they made a mistake in re-birthing Icy when she died she was pregnant and and she was carrying her baby's soul in her abdomen when she died. And then gods granted her a re-birth, and the baby continued to grow, because the infant was not ordinary. It was the child of the powerful Asard.

After realizing this, the gods went insane. The gods came down to Icy and explained that the baby got into her stomach by missteps while creating her, they asked her that they would remove the baby from her stomach , but she refused she had already begun to develop thoughts and emotions for her baby. The gods and Tom chased her down she went running and encountered Fresaiz at some where and she implored him for help. Then later realizing this he got his new expectations to bring Asard back by raising Asard's child power and he managed to escape with her from there.

However, Tom led the divine beings to the Asard's fort as he earlier visited it. The devoted warriors of Asard strove with all their might to prevent the gods from reaching Icy Then later imprisoned Tom as a war prisioner and carried him before Fresaiz, and Fresaiz odered the fighters to kill him. One of the fighters raised his sword

"Wait, please don't murder me; if you let me live, I'll give you a secret about God's weakness,"

bargained Tom.

And he revealed to Fresaiz what he had heard about God's immortality and furthermore, he revealed that the Asard's heart had not been crushed and was instead stored in the heaven. After hearing all of this, Fresaiz determined that he must preserve Asard's baby at any cost and bring Asard back by retrieving his golden heart.

While the soldiers were attempting to block gods from the front, Fresaiz took Icy away from the fort's back gate.They travelled a long distance, and Fresaiz stopped at a point, there he created a tree for the first time, and the tree bloomed its flowers, and it Flicked them, and those blossoms dropped down and they grown up as trees again and formed a dense forest ,then the oldest tree of them produced a fruit, and Fresaid hidden Icy inside the fruit.

Also, the gods arrived at there. They caught Fresaid, and they beat the damnation out of him. The Asard's men arrived there and they saved Fresaid. And they tried to prevent divine beings from arriving at Icy. But the gods started burning the trees one by one. but the trees didn't reveal themselves, so the gods burned the oldest tree. And it reviled the divine beings that how horrible they had killed her offsprings. If when there would be no plants there would be no life, it cursed. Thus the plants became fundamental for life, and the oldest tree and Icy, were captured, and divine beings killed her and took her soul to paradise, and afterward all divine beings chose to rebuff Icy for making this wreck and hell was formed to torture her soul. And she was cast into hell, and once her punishment was completed, her soul was annihilated.

Herthaga enquired "What shall we do with her baby's soul?

"The baby of that Asard should never have peace; it should be left between hell and heaven, battling until the creation exists," Tyronk remarked.

Gersella observed this large number of horrible demonstrations of divine beings, the goddess of affection. Gersella's heart broke down when they attempted to torment a child to that degree then she gave the child a boon while all divine beings were watching in the middle of the paradise, she said the child will get his re-birth not only once as well as threefold and divine beings can never kill him, the no-one but who can kill the child is the child, its self.

Later, evil hid into dull places and backwoods, and they fought from there by spreading evilness into the air, and after inhaling it, the living got the feelings of hunger, and tand they began to kill one another for food, and later infected the living with feelings like dominance,jealousy,racism, and so on, which led the living to hunt eachother, be that as it may, the divine beings brought pleasure into the method involved with making children, and in this way the populace radically expanded..Furthermore, it was the last page of the book. Alex was disappointed with the end of the story. He shut the book and went into the washroom While washing his face, he heard that it was not the end. He stopped for a second and thought it was an imagination, so he went to the front room and he sat on the couch of Then again, he heard something from behind, he turned around then he saw those creatures seeming a large number of ones in the slim air and one of them approached and he introduced him self as Fresaid Alex was stunned he couldn't believe what he was witnessing.

"its isnt over and the child got Its first reincarnation was as Rudolf Bitlor, who suppressed population for making divine beings more fragile however he passed on at last and the secound re birth is you Alex,now

You should support us in bringing your dad back, said Fresaid.

Printed by Libri Plureos GmbH in Hamburg,
Germany